THE
PIZZA PIE
SLUGGER

By Jean Marzollo

Illustrated by Blanche Sims

A STEPPING STONE BOOK

Random House New York

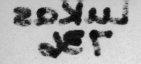

To the third graders, teachers, coaches, sponsors, and pizza makers in Cold Spring, New York—and, of course, to Nonno

Special thanks to consultants Sandy Barton, Noah Kaye, and Claudio, Danny, and David Marzollo

Text copyright © 1989 by Jean Marzollo. Illustrations copyright © 1989 by Blanche Sims. All rights reserved under International and Pan-American Copyright Conventions. Published in the United States by Random House, Inc., New York, and simultaneously in Canada by Random House of Canada Limited, Toronto.

Library of Congress Cataloging-in-Publication Data:
Marzollo, Jean. The pizza pie slugger / by Jean Marzollo ; illustrated by Blanche Sims. p. cm.— (A Stepping stone book) SUMMARY: Billy, the former champion slugger for his third-grade baseball team, is bothered by his very young stepsister's presence at games and feels that she is jinxing him into a batting slump. ISBN: 0-394-82881-X (pbk.); 0-394-92881-4 (lib. bdg.) [1. Baseball—Fiction. 2. Stepchildren—Fiction] I. Sims, Blanche, ill. II. Title. PZ7.M3688Pi 1989 [E]—dc19 88-33379

Manufactured in the United States of America 7 8 9 0

Contents

1. Rat-a-tat Bat   7

2. The Gypsies   16

3. The Spiderweb   22

4. Play-off Game 1   31

5. The Pizza Moon   38

6. Play-off Game 2   48

7. Play-off Game 3   56

8. The Chocolate Story   61

SPRING TOWN'S SPECIAL BASEBALL RULES
FOR MINOR LEAGUE (GRADE 3)

· Each game lasts six innings.
· Coaches pitch the first three innings.
· If you swing and miss, you get a strike.
· If you don't swing at a good pitch, you
   get a strike.
· If you get three strikes, you're out.
· No balls (bad pitches) are called.
· Pitching coaches field the ball like
   regular players.
· Kids pitch the last three innings.

1.

Rat-a-tat Bat

Billy raised his bat and waited for the pitch.

"Hit a homer!" shouted Chris.

"Over the fence for the Slices!" added Rosie. The "Slices" was the nickname of their baseball team. Its real name was Castle Pizza. Castle Pizza was the best pizza parlor in Spring Town. It was owned by Billy's dad.

Billy tried not to think about pizza, Rosie, or Chris. The ball came whizzing through the air. It was high, so he didn't swing.

Everyone was quiet. Nobody said "Ball

one," because balls weren't called in Spring Town's Minor League. The Minor League in Spring Town was for third graders. Only strikes were called in the league. If Billy got three strikes, he'd be out.

"Good eye," said Billy's dad. He was coach of the team.

Mike got ready to pitch again. Mike was Billy's friend, but now he seemed like the enemy. Billy really wanted to hit the ball. This might be his last chance, because the game was almost over. Minor League games lasted only six innings. Now it was the bottom, or second half, of the sixth. There were two outs, and the score was tied five to five against Carol's Flower Shop.

If Billy hit a home run, the Slices would win the game and go to the play-offs. If they won the play-offs, they would become the Minor League champions. Billy's dad would put the trophy in the pizza-parlor window. "That's where it belongs" is what he always said. He really wanted the team to win.

Mike wound up and threw. The pitch came sailing toward Billy. It looked so good that

Billy gave it his super-duper power swing. This was the swing his father had taught him. This was the swing that made Billy the team's home-run slugger. But today the super-duper swing missed. All Billy hit was air.

"Strike one!" yelled the umpire.

"Way to throw 'em, Mike!" said Sally. Billy's friend Sally was catching for the Flowers. Right now she seemed like the enemy too. But deep down Billy knew Mike and Sally weren't really his enemies. He only felt that way because he was having a terrible day. He had been at bat four times and had struck out each time.

Some slugger, he thought.

"Come on, Billy, you can do it!" shouted Billy's mother. Billy didn't look over. But he knew she was sitting on the grass with her other family. This was the first game they had ever come to watch.

The next pitch was way outside. Billy let it go.

"Good eye, good eye," said Joe Spider, copying Billy's dad. Joe Spider was Billy's mother's new husband. His real name was Joe

Snyder, but Billy called him Joe Spider because he was tall and gangly. Billy's mom and Joe Spider had a bratty eighteen-month-old daughter named Lily.

Come to think of it, how come she was so quiet all of a sudden? Forget it, Billy told himself. Don't think about Lily now. Concentrate on Mike's next pitch. Here it comes—right down the pike—nice and slow and ripe for the picking. Billy swung as hard as he could—and missed.

"Strike two," called the umpire.

"All we need is a hit," said Billy's father. His voice was tense. "You don't have to kill the ball."

Billy knew what his father meant. If Billy hit a single, then his teammate Chris would be up. If Chris got a hit, Billy could run to second or third. Then Rosie would be up. If she got a hit, she could send Billy home. Billy's father called this kind of playing "manufacturing" runs. But Billy didn't want to manufacture a run. He wanted to hit a home run and get the game over with. He wanted to be the hero.

"Hit-a-hit-a-hit-a-hit-a-hit!" *That* was his half sister Lily. *That* was the sound that had bothered Billy each time he had been up at bat. "Hit-a-hit-a-hit!" Lily's cheer sounded like a machine gun. It was jinxing him—he just knew it.

While Billy was thinking about Lily, he forgot about the game. The next pitch whizzed right past him.

"Strike three!" yelled the ump.

Billy was out for the fifth time in a row. He lifted his bat in the air and started to throw it.

"Not again!" said Sally.

Luckily Billy heard her. He had already thrown the bat once. The umpire had given him a warning. If he threw it again, he would be kicked out of the game. Billy dropped the bat and kicked the ground with his cleats.

Because the score was tied, the game went on. In the seventh inning Castle Pizza won on a homer. It was hit by Billy's teammate Sam. Everyone except Billy was really happy and excited.

Billy's dad was so pleased that he invited both teams to the pizza parlor for free pizza. Billy sat in a corner booth and started tearing a napkin into shreds. Rosie, Sam, Chris, Mike, and Sally got their pizza slices and crowded into the booth with him. They didn't notice how upset Billy was.

"Pass the cheese," said Rosie. She was especially happy, because she had been the winning pitcher for the Slices.

Billy gathered the shreds of paper into a little pile.

"I said, 'Billy, pass the cheese,'" said Rosie. "What's the matter with you, anyway? Why aren't you eating?"

Billy didn't answer.

"Every time he was up, he struck out," said Chris.

"At least you won," said Sally. "And you get to go to the play-offs. Doesn't that make you happy?"

"Everyone goes through batting slumps," said Sam.

But not everyone has a half sister who jinxes you when you're up, thought Billy. Suddenly he had a terrible thought. What if his mother brought Lily to the play-off games?

"Let me out," said Billy.

Billy's friends let Billy out of the booth. Then they went back to eating their free pizza. Billy went behind the counter to see Nonno.

"*Nonno*" is the Italian word for "grandpa."
Billy's *nonno* had come to America from Italy
when he was young. Even though he'd been
living in America for nearly fifty years, he still
didn't speak English very well. But Billy
understood Nonno, and Nonno understood
Billy, even when Billy didn't speak.

"Tesoro, what's the matter?" asked Nonno.
"*Tesoro*" is the Italian word for "treasure."
Nonno always said that having a grandson was
like having a treasure.

"Nothing," said Billy, pouring himself a big cup of root beer from the soda machine. Being the only kid who could get his own soda usually cheered Billy up. Not today.

"I stunk," he told Nonno.

"You did fine," said his father. He was slicing a fresh pepperoni pizza. "Everybody slumps sooner or later. Don't even think about it. You'll do fine in the play-offs."

"No, I won't!" said Billy. Then he raced out the back door of the pizza parlor.

2.

The Gypsies

When Billy's parents had divorced, Billy and his father moved into Nonno's apartment above the pizza parlor. There they had a kitchen, a living room, and two bedrooms. One bedroom was for Nonno, and one was for Billy and his dad. Billy didn't like sharing a room with his dad because his dad snored at night. But there was nowhere else for Billy to sleep.

Then one day Billy had a brainstorm. He asked his dad if he could use the kitchen for a bedroom.

"You can't sleep in a kitchen," his father said.

"Why not?" said Billy. "We never use it. We cook and eat in the pizza parlor."

"It's a good idea," said Nonno. "We move out the refrigerator and move in Tesoro's bed."

And that's just what happened. Now Billy had his own sink for brushing his teeth, and plenty of counter space for his baseball cards and books. On the front of each kitchen cabinet he hung a baseball poster. He also had a little TV on the unplugged stove.

But that night, when Billy was upstairs in his kitchen bedroom, he didn't want to watch TV or read about baseball or sort through his baseball cards. He didn't even want to take off his baseball clothes. Billy took off his cleats and climbed into bed with his clothes on.

There was a light knock on the door. Billy knew who it was.

"Come in," said Billy.

"Why you in bed?" asked Nonno.

"I'm tired," said Billy.

"Me too," said Nonno, sitting down on the

edge of the bed. Nonno rubbed his face and looked old.

"I might run away," said Billy.

Nonno nodded.

That was the thing about Nonno. Billy could tell him anything. He could tell him he hated his friends and that he stunk at baseball. Nonno wouldn't disagree or agree. Instead he would tell a story about growing up in Italy.

"I might run away," said Billy again, waiting for the story to begin.

"Otello ran away when he was your age," said Nonno, getting a faraway look in his eyes. Otello was Nonno's younger brother. He got in a lot of trouble. Nonno's best stories were about Otello.

"Where did he go?" asked Billy.

"To the Gypsies," said Nonno.

"What are the Gypsies?" asked Billy.

"People who travel from place to place," said Nonno. "They live in Gypsy wagons. One summer they came to our village with a merry-go-round. Otello loved the merry-go-round. He rode it every day. One day he hid in a Gypsy

cart. He say to me, 'You go home alone.' "

"What happened?" asked Billy.

"When my father don't see Otello, he ask me, 'Where's your brother?' I burst into tears and tell him. Papa jumps on his bicycle and rides to the police. The police have bicycles too. They all ride to the Gypsy camp and find Otello. He is washing the monkey cage. He tell the Gypsies he work for nothing so he can ride the merry-go-round."

Nonno began to laugh.

"What's so funny?" asked Billy.

"Papa make Otello sleep in the pigpen with the pigs," said Nonno.

"Did he ever run away again?" asked Billy.

"Never, never, never," said Nonno. Then he bent over and kissed Billy on each cheek— Italian style. "*Buona notte,* Tesoro," he said.

"*Buona notte,*" said Billy. "Good night." After Nonno left, Billy got up and changed into his pajamas. Then he climbed back into bed, because he still didn't feel like doing anything. He lay in bed and pretended he was sleeping with pigs. He couldn't imagine what it was like. And he wondered if Nonno's story was true.

Billy heard Nonno watching a game show in the living room. He heard his father opening and closing the cash register downstairs. He heard the kitchen clock ticking and people walking by outside. But the loudest sound of all was in Billy's mind. It was Lily's rat-a-tat cheer. He heard it over and over again: "Hit-a-hit-a-hit-a-hit!"

What if Billy never hit the ball again?

3.

The Spiderweb

Sunday morning Billy went to church with his father and grandfather. When church was over, Billy kissed them good-bye. Billy's mom was waiting for him in front of the church. Every Sunday she picked Billy up and took him to her house for the day. She lived in the next town.

Lily was sitting in a car seat in the middle of the front seat. Her nose and lips were all red and wet from having a cold. Without a word Billy climbed in next to her and put on his seat belt. He could hear Lily's raspy breathing.

"Hi, love," said his mom. She leaned over and gave Billy a hug.

"No!" said Lily, pushing Billy away.

"But I thought you couldn't wait to see your big brother," said Billy's mom.

Lily looked at Billy and sneezed all over him. Billy wiped his face. Then without his mother seeing him, he stuck out his tongue at Lily.

Lily's eyes grew big and round. Billy made another mean face at her.

"No!" said Lily. She coughed. Her cough sounded like a dog's bark.

This time Billy made a monster face at her. He used two fingers to pull his mouth wide apart and two more to draw his bottom eyelids down.

"No!" cried Lily again.

Billy couldn't help laughing. Unfortunately, Lily started to laugh too. She thought Billy was playing a game with her. "Mo! Mo!" she cried. "Mo" was Lily's word for "more."

Billy turned and looked out the window. Playing with Lily was the last thing he wanted to do.

"Mo!" shouted Lily, laughing and clapping her hands.

Billy's mother laughed too and said, "Nobody makes Lily laugh the way you do, Billy. She just loves you."

Blueberry pancakes, scrambled eggs, orange juice, and chocolate milk: Billy's favorite foods were waiting for him at his mom's house.

"Aren't you hungry?" asked Joe Spider, who had done all the cooking.

"You're usually hungry after church," said Billy's mom.

Billy put one small pancake on his plate and poured syrup over it. He cut off a bite and put it in his mouth. Everyone was looking at him. Billy swallowed hard. "I guess I'm not hungry today," he finally said.

"Mo!" said Lily, who had eaten three huge pancakes with her hands, which were all sticky. Her nose was running, and she had blueberries plastered on her cheeks and hair.

"You don't have to eat if you don't want to," said Joe Spider. "I have an idea. Let's have a catch. I bought a new glove after the game yesterday so we could play ball together today."

"Okay," said Billy. But he didn't want to have a catch with Joe Spider. He didn't want them to be friends. He and Joe went outside to the backyard and threw the ball back and forth. Joe Spider's arms looked longer and longer as he threw the ball. They seemed like spider arms spinning a web around Billy.

"I'm too tired," said Billy, fumbling the ball on purpose.

"Maybe you've got the same bug that Lily has," said Joe. "You'd better go inside and rest."

Billy lay down on the couch and watched cartoons. His favorite show was on. It was about superdogs who fight evil monsters from outer space. All the Superdogs except one were trapped in a cave that was starting to crumble. Billy was so busy watching TV that he didn't see Lily sneak up on him. Suddenly she jumped up and smacked him on the belly.

"Hey!" cried Billy.

Lily still had syrup and goo on her hands. Now there was syrup and goo on Billy's shirt.

"Get out of here!" he yelled.

"Please don't shout at your sister that way," said Billy's mother, coming into the room. She looked at Billy and saw that he was upset. "What's the matter?" she asked.

Billy didn't answer.

"I'll tell you what," she finally said. "I'm

going outside to garden. Why don't you both come out and help me? You could dig some holes."

"Nah," said Billy. "I want to watch TV."

"All right," said his mother. "Then Lily can come with me. Or she could stay inside with you. Would you like to keep an eye on her?"

All of a sudden Billy felt hungry. "Can Lily and I make peanut-butter playdough?" he asked. "I'm starving."

His mother sighed. "But we just had brunch! How come you weren't hungry then?"

"I just wasn't," said Billy. He smiled at Lily and said, "Lily and Billy make peanut-butter playdough?"

"Lily! Billy!" shouted Lily, clapping her hands.

"She really wants to make it," Billy told his mother. "I think she's hungry too."

"Oh, all right," said Billy's mother with a little smile. "But please don't make a mess."

Billy washed his hands with lots of soap in the kitchen sink. And then he washed Lily's hands the same way. He didn't want the icky goo on her hands getting into his peanut-butter playdough.

"Keep your hands in your pockets," he told her.

Lily did just as she was told. She watched as Billy put one cup of peanut butter, one cup of powdered milk, and a half cup of honey in a mixing bowl, and then mixed the ingredients together with his hands.

"Smells good," said Billy.

"Mells good," said Lily.

"Stop copying me," said Billy.

"Dop copy me," said Lily.

Billy took a little ball of playdough and put it on a paper plate in front of Lily. "That's for you," he said. "You can touch it."

Lily poked her ball with one finger.

"Go like this," said Billy. He took a big wad of dough and rolled it into a ball. Then he flattened it with his fist on his own paper plate. "This is how I make pancakes," he said. Billy rolled up the pancake and ate it. "Yum-yum."

Lily flattened her ball and ate it too. "Yum-yum," she said.

Billy gave Lily another little ball and himself another big one. He flattened his ball and added eight long, thin legs to it. "Look, I made a spider," he said to Lily.

"Pider," she said.

"Eat spider," said Billy, putting it in his mouth.

"Eat pider," said Lily. She ate a piece of dough too. Her cheeks, hands, and hair had playdough all over them.

Billy bent down and looked very seriously into Lily's eyes. "When I play baseball, don't say 'Hit-a-hit-a-hit-a-hit.' Okay?"

"Hit-a-hit-a-hit-a-hit!" cried Lily, smacking both her hands hard against Billy's face.

"Ow!" he shouted. "You little pest!" His face stung.

Lily started to cry. And not just cry. She screamed. Billy's mother and Joe Spider came running into the kitchen. "What happened?" they asked.

Billy felt tears of anger come into his eyes. "Lily hit me," he said.

"Did you hit her first?" asked his mother.

"No!" said Billy. "Why do you always think everything's my fault? She starts everything. She's bad luck."

He wanted to add, "So don't bring her to my baseball games anymore!" But he didn't. Instead he stormed out of the room and went back to the Superdogs.

4.

Play-off Game 1

Billy sat on his bed and pulled on his cleats. "Two out of three," he said to himself. "Even if we lose today, we can still win the next two games and become the champions." Billy knew he shouldn't even think about losing. He couldn't help it though. What if his mother brought Lily to the game? Then he'd never get a hit. And it would be hard for his team to win.

Thump! Thump! Thump!

Billy's father was downstairs pounding on the pizza-parlor ceiling with a broomstick.

"I'll be right down!" shouted Billy. He grabbed his cap and raced down the stairs.

"Tie your shoes," said his dad. "I'll be outside in the car. Did you eat?"

Nonno held out a slice of pizza with meatballs. Billy's favorite. Nonno had it all ready for him. It was just right—not too hot and not too cold.

"Thanks," said Billy, chomping it down.

Nonno held out a carton of milk and a chocolate bar.

"Thanks for that, too!" said Billy. He headed for the back door.

"I remember the first time I ever ate chocolate," said Nonno. "I was nine years old."

"Really?" asked Billy. He sipped his milk and waited for the story.

"No time," said Nonno. "You gotta go. I tell you late."

Billy smiled. No matter how many times he had told Nonno to say "later," he always said "late."

"See you late," said Billy, running out the door.

"Good luck," called Nonno.

* * *

Billy and his dad rode in silence to the game. Billy knew that his father was nervous before games.

Billy turned on the radio. One of his favorite songs was playing. He whistled along with it, slapping his fist into his glove to the beat. They rode all the way to the game that way.

As they pulled into the parking area by the field, Billy looked all around for his mother's car. He didn't see it anywhere. What a relief!

"I'm going to change the batting order," said his father. "You'll be up after Sam. That way if Sam gets a hit, you can advance him to the next base. That okay with you?"

"Sure," said Billy.

"Great," said his dad. "Let's go."

Billy knew his dad had changed the order because Sam had been batting better than he had. But he didn't care. Without his half sister to bother him, Billy would show his dad that he was a slugger again.

In the play-offs Castle Pizza was playing Ron's Gas Station. Castle Pizza was up, and

Billy's father was pitching. In the Minor League in Spring Town, coaches pitched to their own teams for the first three innings. They did this because they were better pitchers than the kids. Not many third graders could pitch a hardball overhand with much control. The coaches pitched to keep the game moving and help the batters get hits.

When Billy came up to bat for the first time, he felt pretty good. His mother, Joe Spider, and Lily hadn't come to the game. And Billy knew his father would give him nice easy pitches to hit. He gave everyone good pitches to hit.

The score was zero to zero. It was still the first inning, and there were two outs.

"Come on, Billy," shouted Rosie.

"You can do it," added Chris.

The pitch was on its way, and it was a beauty. Billy swung and hit the ball hard. But he hit it straight at his father, who caught it. He had to catch it. That was the rule. Pitching coaches had to field balls that came at them. Billy was out.

"At least you connected," said Sam, as

Billy sat down on the bench.

"Yeah, right," said Billy.

The next time Billy was up, it was the third inning, and his father was still pitching. The Gas Pumps were ahead five to three, but there were still four innings to go. And now the Slices had a good chance to catch up. There were two players on base. Rosie was on first and Chris was on third. And there were no outs.

"Come on, slugger!" yelled Chris. "If you hit a home run now, we'll be ahead six to five!"

As he walked to the plate Billy hoped his slump was over. He was playing a good game on the field. He had caught two fly balls in center field. And without his half sister to bother him, he was going to hit one over the fence. Billy grinned at his dad.

His father threw the ball. It wasn't the right pitch for Billy. So Billy didn't swing.

"Strike one!" yelled the ump.

"Are you kidding?" asked Billy. He was disgusted, but he didn't yell at the ump. If he did, he'd get an automatic out.

The next pitch was on the way. It was low.

Billy didn't swing, and the ump didn't call it a strike.

The next pitch was low too. Again the ump didn't call it a strike. Maybe Billy's father was too tired to throw any more home-run pitches. But the next pitch was good. Better than good. Billy swung as hard as he could. He missed.

"Strike two!" yelled the ump.

Now Billy had a two-strike count. Billy had often hit home runs when he had two strikes. He started to feel excited. But just as Billy got ready for the next pitch, he heard it: "Hit-a-hit-a-hit-a-hit!"

Lily! Billy swung at the air. He was out. And he was furious. He glared over at the sidelines. There they were. His mother and her other family. They were all waving. Billy didn't wave back.

Castle Pizza lost the first game of the play-offs. The final score was eight to three. Not only did Billy stink, the whole team stunk. And no one came to the pizza parlor after the game.

5.

The Pizza Moon

When Billy awoke, his kitchen bedroom was bathed in silver moonlight. Outside his window was a moon as white and round as stretched pizza dough waiting for sauce. Billy sat up and rubbed his shoulders. He was glad to be in his kitchen bedroom. He had dreamed he had struck out again.

Billy looked at his clock. It was five o'clock in the morning. He heard noises in the kitchen down below. Nonno must have gotten up early. Billy put on some jeans and a shirt and went downstairs. In the pizza parlor Nonno was making pizza dough for the day. His face, hair, and clothes were covered with flour. He looked like a pizza-parlor ghost.

"Buon giorno," said Nonno. "How are you today?"

"Miserable," said Billy, climbing up on a stool. "I hate my half sister. She's bad luck. She makes me strike out."

Nonno poured Billy a glass of milk and set it before him. "Otello hated our little sister Anna," he said. "One day he climb up on the roof and throw little stones on her head. My father was very mad. He made him sleep in the pigpen again."

Billy wondered if Nonno was telling the truth. "What is it like to sleep in a pigpen?" he asked.

"Mud," said Nonno. "Very wet. Very cold. Pigs."

"It seems like a mean punishment," said Billy.

"You think he had to sleep in the mud with the pigs? No. He slept in the hay," said Nonno. "In a bin. You think my father would let one of his children sleep in the mud?"

Billy laughed. It was nice and warm in the pizza parlor. He watched Nonno divide the pizza dough into big round balls. They were bigger than softballs. He set the balls in rows on a large, floured board.

"I hate baseball," said Billy.

Nonno nodded.

"I can't play it anymore," said Billy.

Nonno shrugged.

Billy wondered if his grandfather would tell the chocolate story now. But instead Nonno asked, "You want to be good at something? I teach you to be best pizza maker in the family. Here. Catch."

Nonno tossed a ball of dough to Billy. Billy caught it in the air with both his hands. It was soft and fluffy like a pillow.

"Knead it like this," said Nonno. He put the dough down on a freshly floured marble slab and punched it with his fists.

Billy put his dough down next to Nonno's and copied his grandfather's motions.

"You feel like punching someone?" said Nonno. "Punch the dough."

Billy thought of Lily and punched the dough. He punched it for Joe Spider too, a little harder. "Did Otello like to punch pizza dough?" he asked.

"Otello best pizza maker in Italy," said Nonno. "Now pick it up and keep punching it. Like this. Stretch it with your fists."

Billy picked up his dough. It sagged on his fists like a wet washcloth.

"Punch it up!" said Nonno. His dough was getting flatter and bigger and rounder. *"Via, via, via, su!"* he sang. *"Via, via, via, su!"* He tossed the dough into the air each time he said "su." Billy knew that *su* means "up" in Italian.

Billy tried to stretch his dough. He tried to turn it around in his hands. But his dough kept flopping onto the counter.

"I can't do it," he said.

"Sure you can," said Nonno. "Try again. Like this. *Via, via, via, su!*" Nonno looked like a crazy singing ghost.

Billy picked up his dough again. He stretched it with his fists lightly and quickly. The dough stayed in the air. Billy started to spin it around. *"Via, via, via, su!"* he said, tossing his thick pie in the air. He caught it with his fist and tossed it again.

"Bravo!" said Nonno. "Now together! *Via, via, via, su!"*

Both Billy and his grandfather tossed their doughs into the air. Then Nonno set his circle of dough gently onto a big, floured paddle. Billy kept spinning his.

"Throw it here!" said Nonno.

Billy let his dough go flying. Nonno caught it and spun it around in the air. Billy's thick circle became bigger and thinner. Nonno dropped it onto another floured paddle.

"Perfetto," said Nonno. "You hit ball like you make pizza, and you be slugger again."

"I could do it because Lily wasn't here," said Billy.

"Lily? What does she have to do with it?"

As the moon faded from the morning sky, Billy told Nonno the whole story.

A while later Billy's father came downstairs. "What smells so good?" he asked. On the counter was a big round pizza covered with cinnamon and sugar. Billy and his grandfather were eating it for breakfast.

Billy's father poured himself a cup of espresso coffee. He sat down at the pizza-parlor counter with them. "Pizza-moon pizza," he said. "I haven't had that in twenty-five years."

"What's Pizza-moon pizza?" asked Billy.

"Pizza-moon pizza is made when the pizza moon shines in the sky," said Billy's father.

"It can only be made by a grandfather and his grandson. When I was your age, Nonno's father and I made it. One day, your son and I will make it."

"Where will Nonno be?" asked Billy.

"Don't worry about me, Tesoro," said Nonno. "I'll be the pizza moon."

Billy had a sharp feeling in his throat. He put his arms around his father and grandfather. And they each put an arm around him. The three of them sat close together in the pizza parlor.

After a few minutes Nonno said, "Something bother Billy."

"He'll hit again," said Billy's father.

"More than that," said Nonno.

Billy's father looked at Billy.

"Can you ask Mom not to bring Lily to the game?" said Billy.

His father was surprised. "I don't understand," he said.

Billy told his dad about Lily's rat-a-tat cheer.

His father shook his head. "I can't tell your mother not to come," he said quietly. "Besides, ballplayers have to get used to sounds. They learn to ignore them."

"I can't ignore Lily," said Billy. "She's bad luck."

"Then here's what I suggest," said his father. "Call your mom and tell her what you told me."

"Mom?"

"Hi, Billy! How are you doing? How's school?" asked Billy's mom. She sounded happy to hear from him.

"Fine." Billy couldn't say more.

"Are you okay? Is something wrong?" asked his mother. Now she sounded worried.

"Nothing's wrong," said Billy. "At least no one's hurt or sick."

"But you're upset. What's the matter? You can tell me."

Billy took a deep breath. "Lily bothers me at games," he said. "She makes too much noise. I think she jinxes me."

His mother didn't say anything for a minute. Then she said, "Are you saying you don't want us to come to the next game?"

"I guess so," said Billy.

There was a long silence.

"Okay, then," said his mother. "Whatever you want is fine with us." But Billy could tell she felt sad.

6.

Play-off Game 2

In order to win the championship, the Slices had to win play-off games two *and* three.

It was the first inning of the second game. Billy was up at bat. He was feeling nervous because his mother wasn't at the game. He hoped she wasn't mad at him.

"No hitter! No hitter!" yelled a man. Who was he? Billy looked toward the bleachers where the Gas Pump fans were sitting. A big man was standing up on the top row and yelling. "No batter! No batter!"

Billy couldn't believe it. If that man ever comes in the pizza parlor, I'm going to tell Nonno what he said, thought Billy.

Thinking about Nonno gave him an idea. As the ball came his way, Billy said to himself, *"Via, via, via, su!"* On the word *"su"* he smacked the ball hard. The ball went over the shortstop's head, and Billy had a single.

A single!

It was Billy's first good hit in a long time. Billy stood on first base and looked at the big man. Now he was razzing Chris. "Ignore him!" yelled Billy.

Chris smiled. Then he hit a single too!

In the third inning Billy came up to bat again. The score was now two to one in favor of Castle Pizza. Billy got ready for his father's pitch. Suddenly, he heard the big man yell, "Strike the bum out!"

Billy could tell his father was getting mad. But he knew his father wouldn't say anything. Anyway, Billy didn't need help. He felt lucky.

His dad wound up. The ball came floating down the pike. It was a beauty. *"Via, via, via, su!"* said Billy. He smacked the ball over the third baseman's head. By the time the left fielder caught up with it, Billy was on second base.

A double!

In the fourth inning Castle Pizza was ahead six to three. Billy was up for the third time.

The pitcher threw Billy another beauty.

"*Via, via, via, su!*" Billy smacked a grounder past the first baseman. By the time the right fielder chased it down, Billy was on third base.

A triple!

"Do you realize what you're doing?" asked his friend Beth. She was the third baseman for the Gas Pumps.

"I'm hitting again," said Billy happily.

"Not only that," said Beth. "If you get a home run next, you'll have hit for the cycle."

Hitting for the cycle means hitting a single, a double, a triple, and a home run—all in one game.

"No one ever hit for the cycle in the Minor Leagues," said Beth. "Good luck, even though I am on the other team."

Billy's heart started to pound just thinking about hitting for the cycle. Especially in a play-off game.

His father would be so proud of him!

His mother would be so proud of him too!

Standing on third base, Billy thought of his mother. She wouldn't be there to watch him do it. She would have to hear about it over the phone. Billy knew she had felt sad when he asked her not to come to the game. Now she would feel even worse. She would know her daughter was bad luck for Billy.

Suddenly Billy felt rotten. The next and last time he was at bat, he struck out.

Castle Pizza won the game anyway. Billy's father was so happy that he invited the Gas

Pumps *and* the Slices to the pizza parlor. Everyone came.

Once again Billy's friends piled into the booth with him. Once again Billy started shredding napkins.

Rosie rolled her eyes at Chris. "He's at it again," she said. "What's with him?"

"He's mad because he didn't hit for the cycle," said Chris.

Billy tried to smile. But he didn't feel cheerful. He was thinking about striking out. And he was thinking about his mother. After a while he left his friends and went behind the counter to see Nonno.

Nonno was taking a fresh pizza out of the oven. "What's wrong with you?" he asked when he saw Billy's face. He set the pizza down on the counter. "I thought you won."

"I'm all mixed up," said Billy. "I don't know if I want my mom at the game or not."

Nonno shrugged. "I think you want your mom," he said. "But what about Lily?"

"I don't ever want Lily at the games," said Billy. "Or Joe Spider. Do you think my mom would come without them?"

Nonno cut the pizza into six slices. "Your family is like this pizza," he said. "You got a lot of slices. You got you, me, your father, your mother, your stepfather, and your half sister. Understand?"

"Mom and Dad got divorced," said Billy.

"So? They're still slices in your pizza pie. And you know what? You're a slice in everyone else's pie."

"What do you mean?" asked Billy.

"You're a slice in your mother's pie. You're a slice in your father's pie. You're a slice in my pie. You're a slice in Lily's pie, and you're a slice in Joe Snyder's pie too."

"That's weird," said Billy. But something inside him felt better. And after a while he went upstairs and called his mom. He told her how he'd hit a single, a double, and a triple. He told her how he'd almost hit for the cycle. She didn't know what that meant, so he explained it to her. She listened very carefully. Billy could tell she was proud of him.

"When's the next game?" she asked.

"Sunday," he said. "Two o'clock. You want to come?"

"Just me?" she asked.

"All three of you," he said. All three slices, he thought to himself.

"We'd love to," said his mom.

7.

Play-off Game 3

Play-off game three was bad news. By the time the kids started pitching in the fourth inning, Castle Pizza was losing seven to four. And Billy was having another terrible day. Thanks to Lily's rat-a-tat cheer, he had struck out three times. "I don't care," he told himself, kicking the bench.

But he did care. He just didn't know what to do.

In the fourth and fifth innings, nobody scored. Going into the sixth and last inning, the score was still seven to four. In favor of the Gas Pumps.

Then Chris got a hit. And Rosie got a hit. And Sam got a hit.

Suddenly Billy found himself up at bat with the bases loaded. Great, he thought. Just great. My chance to be a hero, and I'm going to blow it.

"No batter, no batter!" yelled the big man.

"Hit-a-hit-a-hit-a-hit!" yelled Lily.

Why had Billy been so stupid? Why hadn't he told his mother about the cheer? Maybe his mother could have told Lily to stop.

Now it was too late.

"Easy out, easy out!" yelled the big man.

"Hit-a-hit-a-hit-a-hit!" cried Lily.

The big man was rude, but Lily was worse. She may be a slice in my pizza, but she is also a jinx, thought Billy. And her stupid chant is getting louder and louder.

Suddenly Billy realized Lily's chant was coming from Chris. Standing on third base, Chris was yelling, "Hit-a-hit-a-hit-a-hit!"

And on second base Rosie was clapping and yelling, "Hit-a-hit-a-hit-a-hit!"

On first base Sam was doing the same thing! Billy stepped out of the batter's box and looked around. Everyone rooting for Castle Pizza was clapping their hands and yelling, "Hit-a-hit-a-hit-a-hit!" They were all copying Lily to drown the big man out.

Billy looked up at the Gas Pump bleachers. He saw the big man's mouth moving, but he couldn't hear him anymore. Billy looked over to the littlest slice in his pizza-pie family and waved. Lily jumped and waved back.

Billy stepped back into the batter's box and got set. The pitcher threw the pitch. It was outside. Billy let it go.

The pitcher wound up and threw again. It was a fair pitch, but not a great one. So Billy let that one go too.

"Strike one!" yelled the ump.

No problem, thought Billy. He knew what he was waiting for.

The pitcher threw the ball. It was low. Billy wasn't interested.

The next pitch was better, but still not good enough.

"Strike two!" yelled the ump.

All the Castle Pizza fans stopped cheering. All but Lily. "Hit-a-hit-a-hit-a-hit!" she cried.

The pitcher wound up and threw just what Billy wanted. A big, fat, juicy Castle Pizza special.

Billy got set for his super-duper power swing. *"Via, via, via, su!"* he said to himself as the ball came closer. On the word *"su"* Billy sent the pizza special flying. It went way over the center fielder's head. And it went way over the fence, for a grand-slam home run.

8.

The Chocolate Story

Everyone was invited to the victory party at the pizza parlor.

Billy's dad put the new, shiny trophy on top of the cash register. Then he and Nonno kept serving pizza until everyone had a slice. "Don't eat until everyone's served!" said Nonno. "I want to make a toast."

Billy was on a stool at the counter. He had Lily on his lap. His mother and Joe Spider stood close by.

"A toast!" said Nonno, raising his slice in the air. "To Tesoro!" he said.

"Who?" said Chris.

"My grandson," said Nonno. "The pizza pie slugger!"

"Hooray!" everyone cried.

Billy went over and gave his grandfather a hug. He was carrying Lily, so she gave Nonno a hug too.

Lily had pizza sauce on her face, but Nonno didn't seem to mind. *"Caramella,"* he said, giving her a kiss on each cheek.

"What does that mean?" asked Billy.

"Sweet," said Nonno. "Like a candy."

"That reminds me," said Billy. "You never told me the chocolate story."

"Late," said Nonno. "I tell you late."

About the Author

"I love baseball," says JEAN MARZOLLO. "Even though it's a team sport, there are moments when everything depends on what you do. If you get the hit or make the catch, you feel great. If you don't, you feel lousy. The good moments and the bad moments are the same, whether you're a kid or a major league player, and they're the same for everyone else on your team too. All ballplayers share the dream that the next time things will be perfect."

Jean Marzollo has written dozens of books for young readers. She lives with her husband and two sons in Cold Spring, New York. They are all Mets fans.

About the Illustrator

BLANCHE SIMS was quite a slugger when she played on her elementary school baseball team. In fact, she made one of her best friends that way. "She was pitching," Sims recalls, "and I hit a home run. She got mad and then *I* got mad, but somehow we ended up best friends. Later on she would purposely pitch me balls I could smack over the fence."

Blanche Sims has illustrated many books for children, including *Soccer Sam, Cannonball Chris,* and *Red Ribbon Rosie,* all by Jean Marzollo. She lives in Westport, Connecticut.